CURL

CURL

T. O. BOBE

TRANSLATED BY SEAN COTTER

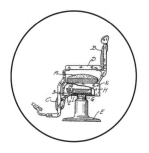

WAKEFIELD PRESS

CAMBRIDGE, MASSACHUSETTS

This book was set in Garamond Premier Pro and Helvetica Neue Pro by Wakefield Press. Printed and bound by McNaughton & Gunn, Inc., in the United States of America.

ISBN: 978-1-939663-42-9

Available through D.A.P./Distributed Art Publishers
75 Sixth Avenue, Suite 630
New York, New York 10004
Tel: (212) 627-1999
Fax: (212) 627-9484

10   9   8   7   6   5   4   3   2   1

CONTENTS

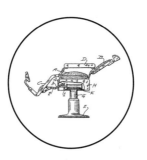

MR. GICĂ
Overview

～

Mr. Gică is the world's greatest barber. He is one-point-sixty-two meters tall and weighs fifty-eight kilograms. He has given haircuts to the fleetest midfielders and highest-scoring strikers. He has cut the hair of the fattest tenors. His barbershop has hosted the longest games of chess. (One, begun eighty-three years ago, in the era of Gică the First, has passed from father to son, and he is still playing it today.)

Mr. Gică is the fastest barber in the world. He holds the world record for sculptural hairstyling and won three Olympic golds in neck massage. But his specialty is the shave. He can remove any beard in one long motion, in waves of ligatures, the way only great artists draw a portrait. It's his signature, and he keeps an example on display in his shop, printed and framed.

ACCOUNT OF WORK PRODUCTIVITY

～～

Mr. Gică's shop has six mirrors on the walls, six sinks, six barber chairs, and no employees. His shop is always crowded and the chairs occupied. Mr. Gică steps from one client to the next, working against the clock, making one move at each. He snips and shaves like this: from morning to evening, he's giving a simultaneous exhibition, and wins every game. He has studied all the scissor openings, he has learned to control the center (that section most exposed to winds), and at the end, when the board is almost empty, he arranges the pieces so that every client walks out pleased and defeated, with head held high.

ABOUT MR. GICĂ, INSANITY, AND DOREL VASILESCU

Some think they're Einstein and they're crazy.
Some think they're Napoleon and they're crazier.
And others think they're made of glass and try not to
    crack,
and others think they're made of paper and try not to
    burn.

Mr. Gică is the world's greatest barber.

Some people think they're doctors,
some inventors,
and some colonels.
And they all try to keep their stethoscopes on their necks
            and their screwdrivers in their pockets
                and their marked-up maps under their arms.
Only once in a while does someone think he's Dorel
    Vasilescu.
Some think they're Socrates and they're crazy.
Some think they're Louis the Fourteenth and they're
    crazier.

But Mr. Gică is the world's greatest barber
and that's what he thinks he is—the greatest barber.

He cuts and shaves six clients simultaneously and never
    makes a mistake.
He has a keen eye and deft fingers.
He is famous and precise.
Someone thinks he's Dorel Vasilescu and is nothing.
He wanders stupidly and wonders what it even means:
    Vasilescu.

Mr. Gică is the world's greatest barber.

Some men think they're Eminescu
and some women think they're Madame de Pompadour.
Some people think they're black locusts
and stand in the yard with their branches up,
waiting for doves.
If you're a black locust, you know what to do.
If you're a sock, you find a foot and sweat together.
If you're the Magna Carta Libertatum,
you go to the basement to avoid sun damage and you try
not to get moldy.
If you're Mihai Viteazu, you stay on your horse
and point your beard at the sky.

But what do you do if you're Dorel Vasilescu
and you think you're Dorel Vasilescu?

Mr. Gică is the world's greatest barber.

The greatest tenors go to him, and the greatest soccer
    players.
They know they are the greatest tenors
and they pull out their handkerchiefs to mop their
    brows.
They know they are the greatest soccer players
and while they wait on the melamine bench,
they retie their shoelaces.
Compared to them, Dorel Vasilescu's hands are way too
    big.
He rubs them together, he sticks them in his pockets.
No one knows he is Dorel. And Vasilescu.

Confidently moving from one chair to the next, Mr. Gică
snips and shaves.
And washes hair. And massages.

Some people think they're Yuri Gagarin and they're
    crazy.
Some think they're Jesus Christ and they're crazier.
Mr. Gică wrote a book
called *Vademecum for Barbers*.
He is the world's greatest barber.
Dorel Vasilescu, dressed in gray, waits his turn,
between a soccer player and a tenor.

Flitting from one chair to the next,
Mr. Gică trims sideburns
and clips rebellious hairs off the neck.

A MAN'S BEST FRIEND

~

Mr. Gică is a man's best friend. Is a man's wife sick? Here comes Mr. Gică's white sleeve for a man to cry on. Did a man just have a child? Before the child leaves the hospital, he gets a nice cut, parted on the left. Does a man have an important meeting? Mr. Gică shaves him to the quick, as only he can. Is a man going to a wedding or a New Year's party? First he gets a massage from Mr. Gică, to improve his blood flow and avoid an apoplexy. Is a man part of an official delegation or greeting someone at the airport? Mr. Gică's dryer puts waves in his hair, adding volume and luster. Is a man giving a keynote at the Academy? He must have Mr. Gică level his sideburns and trim his nose hair. And ear hair. And clip the rebellious hairs off his neck. Mr. Gică is a man's best friend. Even in childhood, a man learns to go to him, at the start of each school year. As best he can, Mr. Gică prepares him for life: he washes his hair, combs him, adds pomade, and a man leaves with calm, confidence, and gratitude for Mr. Gică, a man's best, best friend.

~~~~~~~

Then the students went to school and they all wrote a personal essay what I did on my summer vacation like from Pifs and Rahans spitballs left their heads in a wind the spitballs rose slowly and hit the yellow lampshades hanging in the classroom a wave is when they form letters with their tongues between their teeth a storm is when the teacher walks through and says backs straight the teacher stands and hits her bun on the lampshade heat wave is when the students think looking up to tap their feet tappity-tap the teacher takes the heel off her shoe the compositions were always too short they're supposed to be four pages any shorter means you had an unhappy vacation backs straight says the teacher look you made a blot the notebook is the mirror of the student sunrise is when the page with the battle of Posada is blown by the breeze the student in charge shuts the door you have five more minutes says the teacher and puts the tip of her shoe on her desk her feet smell like the oil from the wood floor hand in your notebooks boredom is when the bell rings and the key around your neck taps your colored shirt buttons.

MR. GICĂ'S LOVE POEM

~

When I was young, I wanted to write you
a love poem.
When I was young, I would see you down the long hallway,
watching television, in a crowd of people I didn't know.
Your legs were crossed.
I was young, and I wanted to write you
a love poem.
I was sad I wasn't Eminescu
or even Sadoveanu,
or someone who could recite, unforgettably, "Hillside Eve."
It was autumn.
You wore your hair up.
I had never seen you with your hair up.
I walked down the stairs
with my eyes glued to your crossed legs,
and without the nerve to say I loved you.
I knew you knew I was looking at you.
I walked down the stairs directly into vocational school.
I wanted to study, for your sake, the most complicated of
*   hairstyles.*

I wanted to invent a unique 'do,
one that would give my love voice.
It was autumn.
Later, in the evening, on the radio,
I listened to Nicu Alifantis sing
"Autumn is here, it's here."
He was singing in the building
where we once were.
I would have loved, have loved
to cover my heart with your hair.
And saturate my pulmonary circulation with its scent.
I lacked any sense of the scent of your hair.
But I would have wanted my heart to pump
the smell of your shampoo
down to the tips of my toenails.
When I was young, it was autumn.
I knew you knew I was looking at you.
And like a fool I left
to learn to make curls (my dumb habit—
complicating things), instead of walking over to you
and saying I loved you.
But your legs were so crossed.

It is possible these were not precisely the words Mr. Gică was thinking. He is the world's greatest barber, and he knows how anyone's hair smells, at any distance, just by the way it shines. Mr. Gică never heard Sadoveanu recite "Hillside Eve," and even if he had, years ago, in elementary school, he's forgotten by now. He is the world's greatest barber and does not have autumnal feelings except toward the herds of children who visit before September 15th. An alp horn? A farmer with a scythe? There's no scythe. Just a razor and scissors. A locust tree? Just a neon sign and mirrors. A church bell? Just a comb knocking the dandruff off against the sink. Only love would have been the same. Or maybe not. Only waiting would once have breathed the same. Mr. Gică is the world's greatest barber. He wouldn't have had any reason to notice, even once, a woman's legs. And even if he did, it was years ago, before he went to vocational school. And he's forgotten.

EYEGLASSES

~~~~~

The hardest thing to endure is the eyeglasses. Not his. Mr. Gică still has good eyesight. But a pair of glasses from a client who didn't put them in his pocket, who forgot them on the edge of the table. Glasses look like a dead man's remains.* Forgotten glasses frighten Mr. Gică. He steers clear of them all day, hypnotized by their empty gaze, hoping the tenor (soccer players don't wear glasses) will come back for them. But no one ever comes back to Mr. Gică for their glasses. At first he would put them in a drawer, and when that filled up, he bought a special cabinet, actually, a metal unit with three lockers: he kept his white work coats in one and tossed the glasses in the

---

* Of course we know no one is buried with his glasses on. You don't even give a dead person's glasses away. No one knows what happens to the glasses of the deceased. They're left in a drawer somewhere, or, if the person was well known, a senator or a historian, then the family devotes a corner of the house to him, placing the glasses among stacks of papers nicely arranged, pens, favorite books, and the pipe of the departed.

other two, one pair after another, dozens of pairs, hundreds perhaps. Every time he cracked the door to throw in another pair, Mr. Gică was frightened. It was a kind of Auschwitz, that pile of glasses, it seemed like all his clients had died, and the dead watched him through their forgotten glasses. But the dead returned to the shop a few weeks later, with new glasses on their noses, and no one brought the forgotten pair to mind, as if they were something shameful, as if they were just something one tossed into a locker, in a little room at the back of a barbershop.

BARBERSHOP NIGHTS
An Eyewitness Account

~~~

Mr. Gică never sleeps.
In the evening, after he closes his shop, he combs his hair,
cleans his instruments, wipes the mirrors, washes the
aprons, and then he rests a little with his fingers crossed
over his stomach, slowly twiddling his thumbs. Once it's
completely dark, he goes in the back
and turns on the sign for the clandestine salon.
Mr. Gică is the world's greatest clandestine hairstylist.

He has six regular chairs and six with hair dryers.
At midnight,
    in lamé dresses
        with bare backs,
            smoking long cigarettes,
                eyes brilliant with belladonna,
they come for Mr. Gică to do their hair:
the wives of tenors and soccer players.
Then he slowly rolls down their velvet gloves,
                        their hose

he rolls down their thighs, and

>   with the zipper of the dress smarting between
>   his teeth,
>   he lets the paleness of their skin stir the night
>   to pity.

Mr. Gică never styles more than six wives a night.
But what style!

>   Logarhythmic shells in all the colors of the
>   rainbow.
>   Pagodas stacking their dreams against each other.
>   Towers that collapse their loneliness together
>   like a telescope.*

The world's most complicated coiffures come from Mr.
Gică.

The most naked

>   most pale

>   >   most brilliant

wives of tenors and soccer players
sit at night in the chairs of the clandestine hairdresser.

Around their hair floats the sticky scent

>   of forget-me-nots.

---

* Cf. "Through the Other End of the Telescope."

To create their coiffures,
the world's most clandestine hairdresser
must peel an orange*
    and tear it into sections.

Mr. Gică visits each of the six chairs in turn,
chewing sections of a blue orange and
exercising his exuviable dexterity.
Then he sends the wives to the hair dryers,
from which they emerge with their auras intact, remade.

At dawn,
when the circles around their eyes sink lower than their
breasts,
the wives of tenors and soccer players
    dive back into their silks, and
    float
    toward the door.
Like a murderous scarf,
he dresses them up to their heads (and down to their
heels)
    in the smell of hairspray.

---

* Cf. "What Mr. Gică Doesn't Know"

                                      T. O. BOBE

WHAT THE PAGODAS DREAMED IN THE POEM "BARBERSHOP NIGHTS"

~~~

Four virgins carry a bloody stretcher through the streets of Rome. On the stretcher is an ear two meters long, with a well-developed olfactory capacity. It is the imperial inspector in charge of prohibited smells. The girls' cleats, quick-quick in little steps, sink into dust up to their ankles. Drops of blood fall to sprout crumpled ears, immediately crushed beneath the crowds of protesters. The inspector heads toward a tavern, where among the sweaty mercenaries, slave traders, and Carthaginian bohemians, Mr. Gică rubs Claudia's feet. On the corner, it turns out that the demonstrators had nothing against the inspector, and were in fact watching Speedy.*

When Mr. Gică exceeds a certain frequency, Claudia begins to cluck and draws from under her wing a sign

---

* Speedy is an Ethiopian gladiator, who escaped the arena thirty-six times via onerous sprinting.

saying OUT OF SERVICE. Then the imperial inspector in charge of prohibited smells enters the tavern. He climbs off the stretcher, flop plop, and states: "Pheromones are stamping here. The smell of their trembling has rattled the head of my hammer all the way from the Coliseum. My most-high synesthesia is revolted. Arrest him!"

Their beards flowing in the tavern smoke, the girls move toward Mr. Gică. Mr. Gică deditur, gallinae proi-iciuntur. Outside the asexual demos stamps and shouts, "Speedy! Speedy!"

WHAT MR. GICĂ DOESN'T KNOW

~

Could this be love?
Will this sunrise ever change its colors?
(La terre est bleue comme une orange)
A man smokes on his balcony.
One thousand six hundred meters away,
diagonally,
through the apartment buildings,
a woman rolls over beneath her sheet.
Could this be love?
The thin, furrowed skin
of her heel.

Her rough hair.
Her pale hands.
The man has never seen her
wrapping her legs in tights in the morning
yet he remembers
her breath before waking.
Her dreams.
Could this be love?
This sunrise will change its colors.
He will smoke.

HANOI

From The Seasons

～～

You can't tell it's spring by the milkflowers. Nor by the swallows or storks, you can't tell it's spring by the cypress buds or cherry blossoms, you can never tell it's spring by a hyacinth of any type.

It comes with the first puppy. It isn't clear whether a schoolboy brings it in his bookbag, whether it wiggles on its own through the door, or it coagulates from the balls of hair that gather in the corners. Usually it is brown with a white spot over one eye and the opposite ear. It quakes in fear of slippers, those foul-smelling and occasionally dangerous animals.

His name is Hanoi.

He laps his milk from a shaving cream bowl.

From morning to evening, Hanoi rolls in the hair, rubs against Mr. Gică's pants, and so on.

This is how electricity is born.

It takes shape as a blue ball, with a characteristic smell pregnant with citrus. Hanoi yaps at it and gives a sniff, waggy-wagging his tail. If it didn't pinch, he would pin it under a paw and gnaw at it. Electricity is beautiful, of course, but it appears when you least expect. Plus, it is quite fragile. If a soccer player comes any closer than a brush-length, it disappears.

Hanoi takes revenge when he can.

If soccer players destroy the electricity, Hanoi chews their shoelaces, or wets on their shiny shoes, if they are tenors.

The end of springtime comes unexpectedly.

When more than the width of a scissor opening has passed since Easter, a customer always forgets his glasses. Dozing under their lenses, Hanoi suddenly lights up. He is so worn out by everyone's love that he barely sparks once when Children's Day lifts him into the air, tethered to four blue balloons.

BE MY NAME *BARBERSHOP*

~~~

My name could be anything.
A woman walks to work in the morning
            and passes her hand through her hair.
My name did not necessarily have

                        to be Gică.
I see her through the shop window,
I sit in the fourth chair and

                looking in the mirror
I see her cross through the name of the barbershop,

            B A R B E R S H O P .
A woman walks in the morning,
I smoke.
Her name could be anything.
My name crosses though my customers' haircuts
and their ladies' nocturnal coiffures.
If she ever turned her head toward the window and read

            B A R B E R S H O P ,
she wouldn't see anything inside except a shadow,

                    a careless outline
and she would rush on.
Her name and my name could be anything.

WHY HAIR NEVER ROTS

~~

Because a person ought to leave something behind, something so sincere it couldn't seem at all calculated, that comes from within and will be stirred by any breath of fear or love.

And because the seborrheic masses on which it feeds are nothing but balls of loneliness, trembling as they rise from the souls of soccer players and tenors.

Because, after Mr. Gică's death, his hair will grow a little, proving its independence, showing that its parallel life is a little out of synch, like the sound in a satellite transmission.

ANATOMY LESSON

~~~~~

The bicep is an important muscle. You can tell a real man by his biceps.

The tricep, just as telling, and the deltoid should make a crease.

The latissimus dorsi keeps the shoulders straight.

The pectorals inflate the shirt, and the abdominals, separated by furrows, attract the eyes.

Mr. Gică's most developed muscles are his piloerectors. Because they contract at the slightest breath of fear or love. Because they contract when they see a pair of glasses or when Hanoi rubs against his pants or when the ember of his cigarette nears the filter.

The bicep is an important muscle. Yet Mr. Gică lifted his heaviest weights with the ends of the little strands of hair standing on upon his neck. His shoulders slope gently, but the imponderable burden of melancholy crushed his lean haunches long ago.

Mr. Gică's most effective weapon is gooseflesh. It has protected him from the iron of the cabinet, triumphed over the spongy rinds of oranges, and helped him rule the imaginary empire of loneliness.

Triceps do count for a lot, and pecs puff out the shirt. But in the morning, after the wives of soccer players and tenors have left, Mr. Gică caresses the vinyl and plays "Lucy in the Sky with Diamonds" on his comb.

His piloerectors slide among the mandarin trees, rub the merry-go-round, and knock against the turnstile, which begins to turn. Thus is born electricity. And decoupling itself from a branch, light begins to crystallize on the horizon.

SUNRISE

~~~~

There where no one is looking for me and so what if they were, where the sky is a complementary color and no one is allowed to smoke, there, among great dunes of hair, Dorel Vasilescu carries a canister on his back. One hand pumps, the other holds the nozzle low, he draws eights and s's. From a distance, he looks like a rat-catcher come to execute the little vandals hidden in the clumps of hair, the mounds, the desert of hair as far as the eye can see. His ashen shadow seems, from the horizon, like an insect on its hind legs, cleaning the proboscis that extends from its belly. Dorel Vasilescu walks with the mechanical, slightly limping gait of one scattering seeds. He pumps and sprays everything around him. And along with him, down the furrow he digs, the shining light of dawn approaches. There where no one is looking for me, where a woman dreams beneath the shifting sands of macerated hair, Dorel Vasilescu leaves a bronze furrow behind him, a heavenly path.

HIPPIE CONVENTION
Season

⌇

At the border between sand and sea, seen between the eyelids, a morganatic summer arrives. On one side, minors abandon their buckets at the sopranos' feet, while on the other, they build castles out of hair, protected beneath green bell jars of darkness. In his striped beach chair, Mr. Gică awaits the hippies. But they are asleep, prodigiously wrapped in the quiet of the sea. At the edge of evening, the world's greatest barber lights cigarette after cigarette. "The hippies are coming!" shout the children, and mud streams from their bodies, sweetened with sweat. "The hippies are coming!" sing choruses of pigmented slaves, clanging their silver bracelets. The light thickens, and beyond it, nothing but the scented resin of loneliness. And before it, nothing is fulfilled but waiting, like a last grace offered to love. "The hippies are coming!" sang the brass bands, their uniforms open to the waist. Yet they, in the depths, rocked like clappers in a bell, they tremble, the hippies, stuck in the nadir's candelabra like darkened candles. They, the four, were supported by the hallucinatory cool of distance.

WELCOME ADDRESS FOR THE INCARCERATION OF MR. GICĂ

~~~

I have no wish for followers.
Followers breathe on your neck, which,
if not assbackwards,
is at least disgusting.
Followers step on your steps.
Journeymen are contiguous with apprentices.
Apprentices resemble women.
They always want to make it last.
I, Mr. Gică, built a monument more ephemeral than air.
I, Mr. Gică, he who cuts that which grows
(except the nails)
gave simuls every time.
I, Mr. Gică, he who cuts hair, shaves, and curls
in six chairs,
always fought against time,
which I loved like a client,
I swept eternity,
that is, everything that does not rot
and gets balled up
in mounds

then in hill after hill
that is, hair.
Hair is humanity's greatest enemy.
Because it gets in our eyes.
Because it stops up our drains
and won't let water through.
Because it sticks its strands
into even the tenderest kiss
and makes lovers pick at their tongues
and become disgusted by their own love.
Therefore, sacrificing myself,
I, Mr. Gică,
he who loves all that grows
(except the nails and hair),
the barber who gives simuls,
I killed the apprentices,
because they wanted to repeat what which cannot be
      repeated,
that is, the ephemeral.

UNDER THE BIG TOP

Silence, shouted Mr. Gică. And then the drums began to beat faster and faster and all the lights went out, except the spotlight trained on his work coat.

Silence, shouted Mr. Gică, *I will now give a haircut to a man with a single hair*, and a knot grew in everyone's throats, their heads tilted back to watch the single erect strand, as he balanced with scissors in one hand and comb in the other, as he danced, as he did splits to the front and side, as he washed, dried, and curled the single strand of hair. They held their breath because there was only the cold tile below, no net, and Mr. Gică was balancing a bottle of aftershave on the tip of his nose, and a hairbrush, and a razor.

He was the world's greatest barber and anyone could see he was not scared of heights, there was silence, absolute silence, all you could hear was his comb sliding down the length of the hair and the scissors snip-snip, and at the end, when he removed the cape and brushed him down and when he said, *There you are*, the applause echoed throughout the shop and the client departed with his eyes full of tears.

In their striped uniforms, with numbers across the heart, the prisoners pace around the jail yard. They walk in a circle, dragging their chains, some with tears in their eyes, others with their eyes on the sand. In place of iron weights, their ankles are chained to soccer balls stuffed with hair. They are watched, through a porthole, by the M.G.M. lion. With a razor in one hand and bangs in the other, Mr. Gică stands in the center of the circle and directs the prisoners in a clear voice. He gives them exercises—to jump through a ring of fire, to seesaw on a plank laid across a barrel—but the big fun comes when the laggard has to open his jaws and put a curling iron inside. When this number is over, the last digit is erased from Mr. Gică's heart. From the watchtower, hand in hand, like worker and kolkhoz woman, Dorel Vasilescu and Vera Muhina order the cast to fall in for roll call.

THE SECRET POLICE SEARCH FOR THE SECRET OF SUCCESS

~~~

Four hirsute damsels in long leather jackets stand beneath the canopy. They have tucked their beards into their belts, over their navels, so they won't get quite so wet. It's raining, it's dark. On their hat-brims, Molliensia Sphenops and Hiphessobrycon Innesi perform erotic dances. The four damsels, aspirants to the rank of Commissioner, stake out the barbershop window.

They hear an engine, then an unacknowledged desire passes before them, at the wheel of a silver Citroën. It's still raining.

The four damsels speak into transmitters hidden in their pipes. With their hands on the guns stuck in their belts, they go into the shop, making the bell ring above the door. (Their names, of course, are Cornelia, Cornelia, Cornelia, and Cornelia.)

Cornelia hangs back to watch the exit.

Cornelia and Cornelia take up posts on either side of the door to the back of the shop, while Cornelia rummages through the drawers, tossing combs, scissors, and towels onto the floor.

Cornelia and Cornelia force the door, they enter the blue jungle of luxurious solitude and find a metal cabinet painted the indefatigable color of hammered copper.

Outside, in the night, Cornelia supervises the rain. Molliensia Sphenops and Hiphessobrycon Innesi race around the wet crown of her hat.

Cornelia continues to ravage the drawers, then she cuts into the vinyl, yanking the stuffing out of the chair.

Confronting the lock, Cornelia and Cornelia exchange significant looks, then Cornelia takes out her pistol and fires. Their feet are flooded by a mound of eyeglasses.

Cornelia thinks she hears something and takes two steps to the side. It was just a running faucet.

Cornelia picks up a pair of gold frames, diopter 1.5.

Cornelia's hands pick through the bottles of lotion, they find the warranty card for a hair dryer and she's excited for a moment, then throws it into a sink.

Cornelia steps on the lenses and opens the other door of the cabinet. She checks the coat pockets, shakes out the stacks of handkerchiefs onto the glasses.

Cornelia has begun unscrewing the mirrors from the walls. She takes them down one by one, tears away the after-shave advertisements, tosses the framed illustration, removes the cupboards wrapped in melamine, and begins to unscrew the sink mounts.

Water gushes onto Cornelia. Irritated, she wrings out her beard, then pulls a packet from an interior pocket and sprinkles her brim with food concentrate for Molliensia Sphenops and Hiphessobrycon Innesi.

Cornelia and Cornelia find the secret door in the back of the cabinet to the most clandestine hair salon. They call Cornelia and repeat the search operations from the barbershop. It goes more quickly, owing to their practiced facility.

Cornelia, Cornelia, and Cornelia come out. Cornelia questions them with a glance. Nothing. They shrug and walk through the rain.

The lights of the Renault brush against their hurried shadows. The unacknowledged desire changes gears and passes alongside.

Cornelia, Cornelia, Cornelia, and Cornelia melt into the dark. Hiphessobrycon Innesi, ever smaller, revels in her congenital phosphorescence, running circles around the crown, long after a wave knocks Molliensia Sphenops into a gutter.

PAJAMAS

~~~

Mr. Gică's pajamas are very beautiful. Wide stripes—blue and light blue. They have drawings of all kinds of baystrucks, millifizzies, juniperzees, and poppylacies. Mr. Gică is quite proud of his pajamas. He has never worn them because he never sleeps, but from time to time he takes them out of their wrapper to spread them on his bed. His index finger gently traces the chichilichees and the bizibutees and the rizisorees. He kisses the gigglenees and wraps them up again, taking care to fold them exactly along the stripes of light blue and blue, light blue and blue, light blue and blue, light blue and blue.

INDIAN SUMMER

~

The Indians had quite nice war paint and wore feathers in their hair. The heat made them sweat profusely, but they kept singing with all their heart, closely following the lead of Joe Dassin. Love, of course, had died. It was very hot, a torrid autumn, and the chorus of lovelorn Indians mumbled something about a love that lasted a little longer, about the summer that didn't want to end. Disguised as John Wayne, Mr. Gică leaned against the doorframe, cupping his elbow in his palm. *Autumn, autumn is here*, sang the Indian chorus, *Love is one month stronger*. The paints ran together, in thin rivulets, Joe Dassin started to feedback, but their feathers, stuck in the savages' greasy tresses, trembled with emotion like the first time they met. When the song was over, Mr. Gică trimmed their hair with his six-shooter. His bullets whistled through the hair around their ears. He was the world's greatest cowboy, and he discovered that even an Indian summer must come to an end.

FOREST EDGE

From The Seasons

~

Mr. Gică would have loved to own a car. But not to drive. Where would he go? He would have wanted one just to park at the edge of a forest, in the rain, with the engine on, and a woman to rest her head on his shoulder, on his tweed jacket. The woman would weep, tears would run, and the tip of her nose would redden a bit, but not too much, and on the windshield, just like

> her tears,
> would run
> the rain.

Mr. Gică would put his hand over hers and
       touch the handkerchief between her fingers,
Mr. Gică would kiss her forehead,
            her eyelids,
     so she would know what
        —farewell—

         means
Mr. Gică running the motor to keep them warm
       to watch the side windows
              —more so hers—
                   fog over.

Then, when he stroked her hair,
                    she would adjust her silk headscarf
                    and weep,
she would be a woman in his car, who looked toward the
        front, at the road,
her shoes would have leaves stuck to their heels
and her beige rain slicker a little dirt on the hem.
The radio would play a tango,
                    and once in a while,
some news reports,

                    traffic,
                    there'd be a wind.
When the wipers moved,

                    there'd be fog.
                    The two of them there
                    she weeps
                a lock of hair caught on the headrest
                and her headscarf as calm as a clasp.
Like they were in a movie together,
French, obviously.

                                Late in the evening,

Mr. Gică would light a cigarette
            and slowly start to drive,
            and she, weeping,
            would keep her head
on his tweed shoulder.

That's what Mr. Gică would have liked.
To have a car in the rain.
To hear it hiss on the road.

STADIUM

~

From the edge of the field, Mr. Gică watches Dorel Vasilescu. Dorel Vasilescu is wearing a checkered shirt with the sleeves rolled up, a pair of jeans, and sneakers. He holds an electric mower by the horns and leaves a stripe in the grass behind him.

Speedy is on the track, training.
A girl takes her run and leaps into the sand pit.

Mr. Gică is in the stands, right under the scoreboard, he watches Dorel Vasilescu mow the blades of grass and Speedy on top of the blades of grass just after he finishes his laps, how he lies on the blades of grass face up and breathes deeply and glances, still on the blades of grass, toward the girl coming out of the sand pit and going toward the pitty-pat patty-cake.

Mr. Gică sits and watches Dorel Vasilescu. And Dorel Vasilescu rakes the grass into piles and bags it, he crosses the field to the pitty-pat, throws the rest of the lime over them and goes to the locker room.

Mr. Gică sees Speedy lift his head from the eleven meter mark and swing his legs over the edge of the sand pit, he hears the gate creak, opening to let her pass, in white, the queen of the pitty-pat, he throws the switch and the stadium lights shine prettily from the tops of their four pillars.

The eyes of Mr. Gică shine with enchantment, he turns his gaze from the sand pit to the blades of grass and the blades of grass grow quickly, they cover the queen's knees and halfway up her titties, and Mr. Gică sees from above, from the stands, how only the white crest of her head is left, like an eleven-meter mark, toward which Speedy, his bleeding heart in his throat, swims through the blades of grass, with his large black feet, like flippers.

~

What can you see? Mr. Gică in the shadow of a tree, in his white work coat, rotund and humble. In the distance, on the hillsides, villagers pass with scythes over their shoulders. In the foreground, a soprano sings "My Dear Wait for Me." Mr. Gică falls fast asleep. He slides toward a bridge, searching for Lucy, he gets in a taxi with the fifty policemen, he gets out among the plastic day-laborers, and he winks at himself in their mirrors, The sky flares like a camera-flash reflected by the Koh-I-Noor. And in the end Mr. Gică rests inside a crack in the clouds. He pulls the curtain of moon and stars over the birdies in their nests. Good night! Oh, for this kind of barbershop, who wouldn't give their daughter and ten grams of their kingdom!

MR. GICĂ IN THE FOOTSTEPS OF EDITH PIAF

Rien de rien, non, je ne regrette rien.
Not the mornings when I sip coffee in my favorite chair, the
fourth from the door, not the mastery of my hands and the
sharpness of my eye, not even the single motion with which
I shake the white cloths, holding them in the air and mak-
ing them pop.

Rien de rien.

I do not regret the past, my stubborn insistence on learning
a trade (and not just any) to the end of the end, tenacious-
ness, humility, grinding teeth behind a smile of permanent
amiability, pain.

Rien. Je ne regrette rien de rien.

"Monotony, emptiness, expecting nothing new."
Love?
A word those gentlemen invented.
Those soccer players.
Those tenors.

Rien de rien, non, je ne regrette rien.

I sit in the fourth chair, enveloped in my solitude like an old caterpillar who can't emerge from his cocoon of hair to fly. And doesn't want to.

Je ne regrette rien.

I am the world's greatest barber. You ought to kneel when you ask for a haircut. You ought to wet my hands with kisses and erect a statue, to change Piaţa Victory to Piaţa Barbershop, to baptize the boulevards with tonsorial appellations. To weave carpets from the hair I cut and spread them over the airports!
I command it!
To fill the springs of every river with shaving cream and flood the world with foam!
What do you know?
The stars are splashes of shampoo I make when I wash your hair.
You assholes!
The dawns are my razor, and they would not shine so brightly
if I didn't strop it on the black voids
of time
I am the world's greatest barber. I apologize for nothing.

Rien de rien.

Be my name Gică
and be my hands those that barber the light
off God's own cheek
and be my scissors those that trim the wings of angels
who sit in my chairs six at a time.
And I regret nothing.
And I won't howl in the solitude of my barbershop.
And what you see, you assholes, are not my tears,
but drops of pure life
that will explode
and spread into infinity the white handkerchiefs of other
universes.

Rien de rien, je ne regrette rien.

NEW YEAR'S
From The Seasons

⌒

Mr. Gică listens to Ella Fitzgerald, *It's only a paper moon*, cuts out the best cardboard noses with his scissors, curls glitter paper wigs, hangs braided garlands from one corner of his room to another, plugs in the tree lights, puts firecrackers on the heater, adjusts once again the boxes wrapped in little hearts and Santas and trees and reindeer and snowflakes stretched so, so big. He's wearing tails, a bowtie with mauve butterflies, and lilac socks. The champagne is 4°C. Carolers and black lads are heard in the background. Once everything is in place, Mr. Gică sits at the head of the table, forgetting to put on shoes. With his eyes on the clock, he awaits for the hands to superimpose. The scent of oranges rises from his feet, from the peels lain on a newspaper to dry. Ella Fitzgerald sings *How happy I would be, if you believed in me.*

MR. GICĂ (PAGES FROM HIS DIARY)

~~~~~

This evening I sat on my balcony. I wore my white work coat, and I believe I still had a few hairs on my lapels from various clients. A few car windshields appeared in the snow drifts. Even though I was cold, I stayed outside a long time, because I liked (and still do) the little colored lights that the city had strung along the boulevard. The stars twinkle just as prettily, even if they are not so well arranged,* some are clear to see, while others, probably because they are farther away in space or time, are barely visible. I wanted to rearrange them, I looked at the lights, then at the stars, but for all I tried to move the little candles with my eyes, into one arrangement after another, they couldn't be saved.

---

* One of Mr. Gică's hobbies is collecting famous film quotes: "It's a pleasure to look at you," "Love means never having to say you're sorry," "Life is like a box of chocolates. You never know what you're gonna get," etc. This time, he recalled Kristin Scott Thomas, sitting Turkish-style on a dune, a cigarette between her fingers, responding with a vague gesture to the man who came up behind her: "They're so untidy. I'm just trying to rearrange them."

VADEMECUM FOR BARBERS (FRAGMENT)

~~~~~~

Love is when the film ends and they kiss but before that she didn't know he loved her and wanted to go somewhere else and see another guy and he didn't know how to tell her without making her mad but in the end he let her know but she didn't know because she never even thought he might love her and in the end when he said he loved her she realized she loved him too and she didn't go anywhere she stayed with him and they began to kiss and that was it when they fell in love the film ended and they went home.

COMMENTARIES

———

I know for sure it never happens like that. That this is just a movie in a book for barbers, maybe for hairstylists, too. We're never going to go to the movies or kiss at the end or hold hands in the crowd by the exit. In the morning, you're going to pass by the barbershop and see thick, dark lines rising over the plate-glass window like you see on a television. I'm going to trim and shave soccer players and tenors. I'm going to even their sideburns and clean the hair off their necks. I know, my love, that I'm in a different movie, that our names are already scrolling in different credits, I know for sure that in the crowd by the exit, we will be alone.

MR. GICĂ'S REMEMBRANCE OF A LOVE

~~~

When I was young,
I wanted to write the remembrance of a love, about you,
the world's most beautiful remembrance of a love
something like Love Is Not a Crime
or When the Wind Ruffles Your Hair.
I wanted to write the remembrance of a love,
one that would be quoted in everyone's love questionnaires,
in everyone's yearbook.
That's why I would have liked to be with you
on those chilly mornings
when you wrapped a sweater around your legs,
when you stretched your hypotensive fingers blindly
toward the coffee cup,
when you took magnesium to make yourself smart
and when you pedaled quick-quick on the stationary
        bicycle.
I knew you always left the faucet running,
but that hadn't the least importance,
I liked the way you said, "What do I care?"
and the way you bounced your knee when you sat
        cross-legged,

I liked how we met in the morning at the bus stop
and we squeezed into the 135,
and we bought a Vițeluș *yogurt.*
I liked the rings under your eyes
and your nails painted with glitter
just for the fuck of it,
and the way you bit your lower lip
and how you said, "babe,"
I liked it when we read
magazines together like VIP *and* Paranormal Phenomena,
I liked teasing you when you said you're autistic,
I liked using the phone right after you, so much,
because the receiver smelled like Byzance.
I wanted to write the remembrance of a love, about you.
So everyone would know how you said, "I can't believe it"
and how you asked "Really? No kidding?"
I wanted to write the remembrance of a love,
but I could only write the remembrance of an
        embarrassment,
the remembrance of a longing.
The remembrance of a love for you
always hidden behind the remembrance of an
        estrangement,
the way your green eyes hid
behind glasses with green highlights,
the way my white work coat hides
behind the window that says **B A R B E R S H O P** .

LULLABY

⌒

I knew you dyed your hair.
You went to work in the morning
and in my ears
   was nothing but music
     by Goran Bregović.

I knew you dyed your hair.
You could have been in Aesthetics, *on the cover:*
       you were as beautiful
    as an equilibrium of
    supply and demand.
You passed on Pache Protopopescu Blvd.,
  dressed in a deux piéces—
      you were all advantage
      I was all excess.
I would have played the sultan for you:
     I would have named you
     the model
     of flowers painted
     by Georgia O'Keeffe.

I knew you dyed your hair.
                                    Springtime was brunette—
you breathed on my brain
                    and my brain

                                    became a dandelion
            whose fluff

                        was split in two
                        like by a razor
                        like by the music
of Goran Bregović.

MR. GICĂ AND CATABIOSIS

⁓

I gave a haircut to one person, then another, then another.
Then I shaved someone
and then another haircut and a shampoo
and another haircut and a shave.
As time passed, I started to give massages.
The first week in my profession was hard,
the second even harder.
The third week, I gave haircuts, shaves,
and shampoos.
The fourth week, the same.
And the fifth.
I became the world's greatest barber.
I cut the hair of one soccer player and then another.
I massaged the whole neighborhood and the whole country
and the whole world.
I dyed eyebrows and matched the moustaches
and trimmed nose hair.
I cut the hair of one person then another and another.
Day after day.
I trimmed ear hairs, I evened sideburns.
For what?

My days are the same
and my nights are the same
and all my life is a barbershop
where I fold an ear over
to curve around it with my scissors
and all my life is a mirror
where I see myself holding a client by the nose to trim his
mustache.
My entire fortune would fit neatly on a bathroom table
and my love is swept up with the hair.
For what?
I gave a haircut to one person then another and another.
I am the world's greatest barber.
And I keep giving haircuts and shaves
and dusting the neck with talc.
And I give massages.
Soon, I'll die.
Death doesn't scare me. I only wonder
if I will be crushed beneath the mountains of hair
that will rise on top of me.
How light all the hair in the world must be
if a single barber can cut it.
How much foam does he need
to moisten all the beards in the world?
I must die.
Death doesn't scare me. Its barbershop does.
That place where I'll have to give a haircut to one person
then another

T. O. BOBE

then another.
Death doesn't scare me.
But in the beyond, if there's a beyond, are there soccer
  players and tenors?
I gave a haircut to one person then another then another.
And, when I look in the black of my eye in the black of the
  mirror,
I see death in a white work coat
with a comb coming out of his breast pocket.
He is one point sixty-two meters tall and weighs fifty-eight
  kilograms.
He has all the time in the world, and behind him,
through the door marked **B A R B E R S H O P** ,
one person comes in then another then another.

MR. GICĂ'S LAST WISH

While he was still young (about forty years old), Mr. Gică expressed his last wish. The last wish expressed was something like this: *After I die, don't bury me, and please don't burn me up. Better to stuff me. But not with straw— use hair. Stuff air me, as it were. And put me in a corner of the barbershop, in my white work coat, with scissors in one hand and a razor in the other. Put a comb in my breast pocket. Don't worry, it won't scare people. Whoever knew me will know I'm a good person, whoever doesn't will think I'm a mannequin. Don't forget to dust me from time to time. And if possible, recondition me. Like Lenin. Understand? I don't want to be stuck in the ground. Stuff me with hair! Keep me close. And make sure the comb in my pocket isn't made of bone. I want it to be plastic, the kind of teeth that make music when you part a client's hair tenderly.*

ANNIVERSARY

~~~~

Every year, on World Mental Health Day, Mr. Gică is visited by Einstein, Napoleon, Socrates, Louis XIV, Eminescu, Madame de Pompadour, and Yuri Gagarin. Mihai Viteazu doesn't come because his horse won't fit in the barbershop. They each sit in a chair and converse politely, then Einstein takes out his violin and plays a special dedication to the world's greatest barber, Paganini's *Caprice 17*. Very moved, the others gather around Mr. Gică, each holding a pair of scissors. Instead of saying goodbye, they stick the blades awkwardly into his white work coat. After they leave, Dorel Vasilescu arrives and sweeps the hair into a pile, stitches up Mr. Gică, paints his face and reattaches him to the stand. Dorel Vasilescu is the world's greatest taxidermist.

SUNSET

~

Mr. Gică holds scissors in one hand and a razor in the other. He stands in front of the door and watches the blue vein that beats, between two layers of membrane, on the sky's temple, he stands in front of the door, and his shadow stretches, past the threshold, one-point-eighty-three meters. From his pocket a comb half emerges, its teeth thin and close. No woman passes down the street, no schoolboy, and Mr. Gică is the world's loneliest barber. No puppy rubs against his socks. No tenor sings *Adio del passato*. Mr. Gică turns, his long, white tresses reflecting the light once more, then they disappear, sweeping across the tile, into the depths of the barbershop, like an immaculate bridal train.

TRANSLATOR'S AFTERWORD

I have a mug that claims I'm "the world's greatest dad," but that's impossible, puffery. Mr. Gică, on the other hand, is "the world's greatest barber," a title that's too big for the world but fits the book precisely. Lodged in the impossibility of both of these superlatives is a gentleness, a genuine warmth—my daughters for me, Bobe for Mr. Gică. That combination of artifice and sincerity creates the book's surprising charm. A translation is itself an artifice, a substitute text constructed through sincere mimeticism. In the process of translating the book, I followed Bobe's insight that our understanding of artifice depends deeply on our experience of the real, that the world's greatest barber is still a barber in the world.

Bucla was first published in Romania in 1999, when it won a first-book prize (actually it won two, and Bobe had to turn one down). It enjoys a cult following strong enough for two more editions (as half of *Centrifuge* in 2005, and a deluxe edition in 2015).[1] Bobe has worked in theater, film, and television, and he has published a novel (*How I Spent My Summer Vacation*), a children's book (*A Gift from Santa Claus*), and a collection of short stories (*The Contortionist*).[2] He is part of a group that includes Svetlana Cârstean and Răzvan Rădulescu, among others who were part of a weekly writing workshop led by Mircea Cărtărescu. That last identifies "kitsch" as "the main source of inspiration for the group. In Teo's case it tilts toward innocence and fantasy. And 'fantasy' is only one step away from the 'barbershop' (*de la 'feerie' la 'frizerie'*), a small step for man."[3] Cărtărescu frames Bobe's poetry as the heir of major works of Romanian postmodernism. In *Bucla*, Bobe has found a form to explore our emotional investment in apparently shallow, kitschy constructions. Along the way, he has increased my investment in seemingly shallow conversations, such as those I have with my barber.

Cărtărescu calls Bobe "Teo." It's confusing to walk around Bucharest telling people "yesterday I had beers with T. O. Bobe," since his name is a pun and a pseudonym. It's no secret, no Ferrante: "T. O." is a homophone for his name, "Teo," short for "Teodor," as in "Teodor Dobrin." But the false name creates an interesting effect. When you are speaking, you don't have to choose between "T. O." and "Teo"; the distinction only shows up in print. His author's name is precisely designed to function best on his works. Fortunately, he and I call each other by our first names, and perhaps one day I'll know him well enough to call him "T." "Bobe" is the name of his maternal grandfather, who would both spin stories and take him to the barber. Bobe, the author of this book that includes false homework assignments and skeptical academic commentaries, adopted the pseudonym early on, to separate his college persona from his burgeoning literary identity. The story of the name repeats the binomials of the book: study of art and creation of art, speaking and writing, life and literature—artifice and genuineness seem to envelop the world that produced the work.[4]

Perhaps the book has a following among Romanians because of their real-life experience: everyone gets haircuts (except priests). Lots of people thus have uncomfortable conversations

SEAN COTTER

while their body is manipulated by a casual acquaintance. Bobe tells of a haircut inflicted on him when he was nine, when his regular barber ("Emil") was on vacation, and the available barber was slightly soused. Bobe resisted the idea, not because of the booze he could smell, but because he admired the era's long-haired hippies (cf. "Hippie Convention"). The cut was asymmetrical and brutal, so short and ragged that young Teo burst into tears. The barber did the same, refused any money, and Teo's grandfather tried to convince him short hair was better, since hippies smelled like wet dogs (cf. "Hanoi"). Bobe cites this experience with one of the world's worst barbers as an inspiration for Mr. Gică.

The kitsch in *Bucla* is tied to the real-life experiences of growing up in Romania, in Europe, in ways that an English-language reader might not immediately understand. Some typical tropes of Romanian history figure in the book not to invoke historical depth but to evoke the shallow acquaintance with history we acquire in school. For example, Mihai Viteazu is the guy the statue is made of, lots of statues, a guy on a horse. He was the sixteenth-century ruler of much of present-day Romania. The Battle of Posada occurred in 1330, when the Hungarians lost to the Romanians. These types of data are schoolboy kitsch. Mihail Sadoveanu was a twentieth-century novelist—farmers, peasants, kitsch. Mihai Eminescu is the guy on the money, the 500 lei note, more than you'd need for a night out with the "national poet" of Romania. "Hillside Eve" is one of his poems, nineteenth-century Romantic. Kitsch. Nicu Alifantis is a velvet-voiced singer who has set many Romanian poems to music. Kitsch. "Autumn is here" is the first line of a poem by Nichita Stănescu, "Emotie de toamnă," rendered into English by yours truly as "Autumn Love." Kitsch. Dorel Vasilescu, just to be clear, is fictional kitsch, the book's antagonist.

The references expand to include America and Europe. I assume that many of these—Louis Armstrong, Edith Piaf, Paul Eluard, Forrest Gump—don't need explanation. Yuri Gagarin was the first person to orbit the Earth, a cosmonaut, thus, a Soviet. In the United States, we grew up under a different system of kitsch propaganda, one that called them "astronauts," instead. (But this is one of those moments when I wonder about our Greek. *Astro* indicates "stars," a "star man"—so "astronaut" = David Bowie. But *cosmo* is "the cosmos," a word we already have in English—so "cosmonaut" = Carl Sagan, who was not a Soviet.) *Pif* is the name of a series of French comic books, popular in the 1970s, and Rahan is one of the characters, a stone-age scientist and wanderer, a petronaut. The "Worker and Kolkhoz Woman" is a 1937 eighty-foot statue in Moscow, the worker with a hammer and the farmer with a sickle, the emblem of socialist realism, the icon of Soviet film. It was designed by Vera Muhina. The Koh-I-Noor is a big diamond. Children's Day is June 1. World Mental Health Day is October 10. The important fact about these facts is their lack of importance, the way these shallow figures are the context for our lives.

All of these references, since in the end they reference artifice itself, could be substituted in translation with American artifice. Carl Sagan, for example. Or instead of the Battle of Posada, the Battle of Gettysburg. Instead of Nichita Stănescu, Rod McKuen. Noticing that the book would license this possibility is enough. Following through would be a mistake, because to reduce the field of allusion to a single country would distort our insight into the book's international scope. My favorite example is "Indian Summer," where Native Americans, dressed as Indians, face Mr. Gică, dressed as John Wayne, the world's greatest cowboy. Supporting the Indians is the 1970s pop singer Joe Dassin, most famous for "L'été indien." We have Native and Anglo America inhabiting a maudlin song (sung in French by an American of Ukrainian and Polish descent who studied music in Switzerland), confronting a kitschy John Wayne stuffed with a Romanian barber. I suppose we could translate or relocate these multiply rooted references, but I don't know into what language.

In this case, I wondered whether to translate the Romanian into English or into French. Joe begins the 1975 original "L'été indien" with a throaty bit of spoken explanation, to bring the term "Indian summer" into French, "Une saison qui n'existe que dans le Nord de l'Amérique. Là-bas on l'appelle l'été indien. Mais c'était tout simplement le nôtre." International Joe translates this North American season into French, in order to claim it exclusively for himself and his French lover, "tout simplement le nôtre." But there is a competing North American version. In the 1976 English re-recording, Lee Hazelwood tells Nancy Sinatra to recall "that rare kind of autumn that you only find in North America. We call it, 'Indian summer,' but it was quite simply our summer." In other words, the proud Oklahoman translates Joe's discourse of translation into English, in order to usurp Joe's translation. Lee changes "là-bas on l'appelle" into "we call it," and reclaims Joe's summer for himself and Nancy, "quite simply our summer." In these translations of translations, Joe and Lee compete over the North American autumn like Europe over North America, represented in *Bucla* by the figure of John Wayne. The text of Bobe's poem, where cowboys shoot at Indians, refigures this history of colonizing translations.

Lee and Nancy's version, for American readers, is a precise analogue of the kitsch that Bobe's Romanian book enjoys. It's worth a Google. I wavered in the translation of this poem, which in the original is entirely in Romanian. I wondered whether I should put the Joe Dassin title in French, to contour the confrontation more sharply. In fact, the poem references an idea ("love, of course, was dead") that only appears in the French version. Unlike Syd and Nancy, Lee and Nancy's love never dies. A further complication is the fact that the italicized citations in the original belong to neither the French nor the English version of the song. The first quotes the Nicu Alifantis setting of Stănescu mentioned earlier; the second is Bobe's interpellation. In the end, I decided to leave the English translation monolingual, out of affection for the original text.

The trickiest translation problem is the name of the protagonist. It's the first word of the book, whether you count from the table of contents, the chapter title, or the block of text. It's the one word my Romanian friends ask me about, because they know there is no good answer. The original is "Nea Gică." The second word, "Gică," is a name, short for "Gheorgică," which is long for "Gheorghe." A nickname, this time, not a pseudonym. As the man himself states, "My name did not necessarily have to be Gică." So one translation could be "George is the world's greatest barber." But the problem word is "Nea," which in Romanian is a title in place of a title. In this case, it's in place of something more formal, *domnul*, which really ought to be followed by a last name, not "Gică." Usually, *domnul* gets the translation "mister." "Mr. Jankowitz is the world's greatest barber." But who calls their barber "Mr. Jankowitz"? I call my barber "Mr. Bryan," but for many years I avoided calling him anything at all. I'd walk to his chair when he waved me on, sit and be wrapped in a cloth printed with the American flag. He's a great barber, and as a man with curly (rebellious) hair, I know a good cut is not a given. In the same way that Romanian barbers don't wrap their clients in the American flag, this

"Nea" is not a word we have in English. In the end, I was won over to "Mr. Gică" by the way it sounds. (The "gi" is like "gee," and the "că" is like "kuh." Míss-tur gée-kuh.) And it's not a bad thing that the book begins with a Romanian name, the nickname of the diminutive that's longer than the actual name. Mr. Gică is not a real barber, but the book is fixed in a particular unreality that grows out of Romanian reality.

In the end, it is satisfying to me that the book and its translation bring us back to what counts as our reality, our experience of barbers. As I told Teo over some Belgian beer, all of my haircuts in Romania have been unusual, filtered as they were through my foreignness and my miscomprehension. It's also true that the cuts themselves, even with my rebellious hair, have been excellent. My first cut came due a couple months into my first trip, after my language class had had a lesson on "the barbershop." One Saturday, I entered the first *frizerie* I saw, which turned out to be huge, with multiple rows of chairs, all of which were dark. Two chairs sat in a small island of light. At one, an enormous man in a double-breasted work coat snipped with comparatively tiny sheers. His hair was parted in the center and slicked down either side, he wore metal-rimmed glasses the size of two nickels, and his moustache was waxed. He nodded over his shoulder to the other barber, who emerged from behind him like one of Jupiter's tiny moons. She had a simple blue work coat and a dynamic bouffant, short on the sides and long down her back. She coughed quietly and constantly. My language lessons left me as I sat down, so I could only motion how I wanted my hair done. "Are you American?" I was. The larger barber barked at her, "Don't talk to the clients!" But she was very curious, so she leaned closer in and asked more questions and coughed. "It is beautiful there?" Parts were. "Like in *Dallas*?"

He shouted at her again. That stopped conversation until the very last moment I was in the chair, when she brought her face close to mine, almost nose to nose, and said, "Once, I drank too much Coca-Cola, and I vomited." That was the end of the conversation; I paid and left. Bobe thought this episode would make a nice fifteen-minute film.

Sean Cotter
Bucharest and Richardson, 2018

NOTES

1. *Bucla* (Editura Univers, 1999; Humanitas, 2015), Premiul Național Mihai Eminescu pentru debut în poezie. *Centrifuga* (Editura Polirom, 2005). Translated into German by Eva R. Wemme as *Zentrifuge* (Merz & Solitude, 2004).

2. *Darul lui Moș Crăciun* (Humanitas, 2003). *Cum mi-am petrecut vacanța de vară* (Editura Polirom, 2004). *Contorsionista* (Humanitas, 2011).

3. "Viața și opiniile lui nea Gică frizerul," *Curentul*, 18 mai 1999, 4.

4. Romanian readers can enjoy a series of interesting interviews online, and non-Romanians can enjoy the pictures:
https://www.viitorulromaniei.ro/2014/05/07/teo-bobe-scriitor-sa-promovezi-carti-in-romania-e-ca-si-cum-te-ai-apuca-sa-vinzi-caciuli-de-blana-in-sahara/
http://metropotam.ro/La-zi/Interviu-T-O-Bobe-art3644366052/
https://adevarul.ro/cultura/carti/interviu-scriitorul-t-o-bobe-mircea-cartarescu-s-a-parut-unul-cei-mai-buni-profesori-seminar-ascultam-fascinat-1_545096730d133766a85509a9/index.html

Sean Cotter's translations from Romanian have won several prizes, including the Three Percent Best Translated Book Award for Poetry (2013). He teaches translation at The University of Texas at Dallas, as part of the Center for Translation Studies.

SUBVERSE